THE BACKROOMS

MATT WILDASIN

THE BACKROOMS

<u>**MORE BOOKS FROM MATT WILDASIN**</u>

SHORT STORY COLLECTIONS

EDGE OF TWILIGHT

HORRORS UNTOLD

HORRORS UNTOLD 2

HORRORS UNTOLD 3

HORRORS UNTOLD 4

HORRORS UNTOLD 5

DARK WORDS: STORIES OF URBAN
LEGENDS AND FOLK LORE

NOVELS AND NOVELLAS

BAGGAGE

MELANCHOLIA

THE DEMON IN THE GLASS

IT CAME FROM THE SEA

CONTENTS

ACKNOWLEDGEMENTS

Firstly, this book would not be here if it were not for the help and support of my loving and devoted wife and editor, Jamie Wildasin.

I would like to thank my mentors and good friends, Mary Sangiovanni, Somer Cannon, Stephen Kozeniewski, and Brian Keene.

The following is a list of close friends that have always supported my writing and encourage me to keep writing: Will Bacon, Levon Higgins, Jason Thomas, Eyglo Karlsdottir, Shyla Watkins, Steve Clark, Amy Lower, Simon Paul Wilson, Tasha Reynolds, Laurel Hightower, Alexander Bailey, Richard Gerlach, and Gavin Dillinger.

In loving memory of Dave Thomas.

I would like to give a special thanks to my supportive parents: Wayne and Ann Wildasin and Greg and Mary Jane McFalls

Lastly, and most importantly, I would like to thank you, dear reader. Without your support, none of this would be possible.

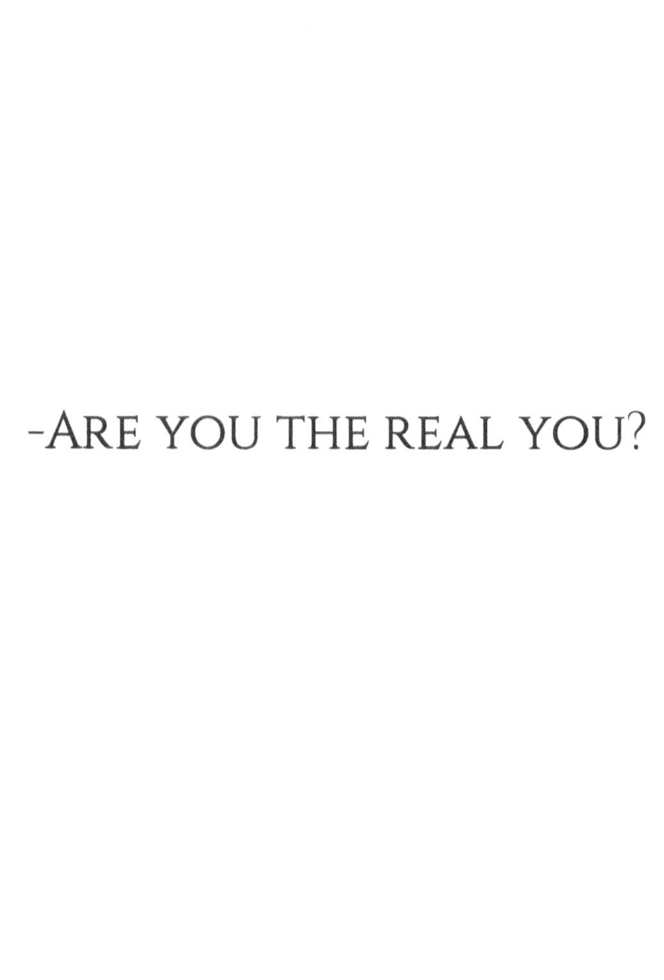

-ARE YOU THE REAL YOU?

INTRODUCTION

This book was a long time coming and it was one of the hardest projects for me to complete. Its life started off a year or so ago as a short story in HORRORS UNTOLD VOL 4. It was a fan favorite amongst readers, and I was asked several times to expand upon the story and was quick to pen the short into a novella. Upon completion, I had the idea of submitting it to some publishers in the hopes to have another release through a small indie press. For a gamut of reason, this book was never picked up and I shelved it for some time, thinking that it was not good enough, or simply doomed. It wasn't until mid-way through 2022 that my wife found the file and decided to read over it. The story that I deemed unfit found love in one reader's heart. She urged me to work on polishing the manuscript and get it out there under my own imprint. It took some convincing; at the time I was in a dark place with the trade and nearly walked away from it altogether. As many of us creatives do from time to time, I felt I didn't have the chops to hold my weight and the sea was so vast that I felt like I was drowning.

My wife hounded me for months to get back on the wagon and make this book my priority. I had several other projects in the works at the time, ones that I hope will see the light of day this year. I did feel overwhelmed by the challenge, but my wife never steered me wrong in our thirteen years of marriage, so I took the plunge.

The work was hard. There were tears shed and laptops slammed shut. This book seemed hopeless, as I said before; it felt like it was a doomed thing from the start. Still, we kept pumping on, fine tuning things, switching paragraphs and cutting out ideas. The tears started to dry up and the feelings of hopelessness began to fade. Then, another hurdle came our way.

On January 7th, at 6:08 AM, my son, Vander Grant Wildasin, was born. It was an amazing gift; one that I still can't believe I am worthy of having, but I am beyond grateful for him.

It was hard prying myself away from him to write. It was even harder finding the time to write, as anyone who's been a parent knows, sleep and free time are a thing of dreams. Still, my wife was there to support me because she believes in my dream and made sure to give me time to work. That being said, it was still damn hard to finish this project. As I type this introduction, the publishing date is only six days away.

If you are here and reading this, I thank you from the bottom of my heart. This book was my novella-sized white whale and a true labor of the love of writing.

Being horror and science-fiction, it was a genre mix that I had never tried before. Despite my amateurish status with the science fiction genre, I hope it shows in the final product that I wanted to do the material justice.

So, if you would care to join me, let's get lost in The Backrooms together.

LETTER 1

Are you the real you? The one that wakes up every morning doing the exact same routine, never questioning life. How do you know none of this is premeditated? How do you know that you're not simply just a cog in the machine? Or a meat suit carrying out menial tasks to serve another purpose? I thought I was real. I thought for years that I earned what I owned and was rewarded for my hard work. Then, one day… I woke up. If you're reading this, then you did too.

That's why I'm writing this letter to whomever may find it—if anyone at all. This is the legacy I plan to leave so that, no matter what happens to me, I will have left behind something to be remembered by.

When I think back to when this all started, I never would have imagined that I'd end up in a place like The Backrooms. In retrospect, I have no one to blame but myself for it, all because I was too curious. I discovered too much and ended up banished here.

Things seemed off back in 1999, when we thought Y2K would wipe out everything. It's funny to think back to that time: everyone getting in a tizzy thinking their toaster wouldn't work or airplanes were going to fall out of the sky. After it came, we all woke up the next day, and everything seemed the same, but it wasn't.

I want people to know who I am and what it was that I discovered that landed me in this hellish place. My name is Greg Smith. It's as vanilla a name as they come for the vanilla life I led. I lived an innocuous life, working in an office building for Orion Industries doing some coding for D.I.Y websites and maintained servers for podcast storage and blog sites. Pretty easy work, if you know what you're doing.

It wasn't until around 2003 that I started to realize weird things happening around me. I started having déjà vu more often, sometimes for entire days. I checked in with doctors, got clean bills of health and was simply ordered to get more sleep. But even sleep became illusive, causing me to lay awake for hours with troubling thoughts. My mind toiled over the strange afflictions I had been suffering from or the unusually robotic, sequential actions of those around me each day as I tried to fall asleep.

Instead of lying awake uselessly, I started spending my sleepless nights researching what was happening to me. I came upon a website called 'The White Cat,' which housed articles and blogs written by several people that claimed to have suffered from similar ailments to my own and started to see this beautiful stray white cat. The cat sightings were not something at the time I had experienced, but it was reassuring to find others that had endured the same things I was—it made me feel less like I was going crazy.

I read on about the White Cat out of sheer curiosity to discover the conspiracies revolving around the little creature. There were claims that the furry beast was a program; a part of this huge Y2 system in control of everything that has been active since the turn of the century. The White Cat was apparently built to seek out the rogue programs, meaning people like us that "awakened."

Coincidentally, as if somehow my searching about on the internet had been monitored, the White Cat was outside my apartment building the next day. At first, I ignored the strikingly beautiful feline and continued about my life. But each day, like clockwork, I spotted the cat walking out of alley alongside the building, it would meow at me a couple of times whilst circling its steps, then, it would put up its tail and walk back into the alley. Just as the articles had warned me about, its behavior signified that it was trying to get me to follow it somewhere. For weeks this went on; the same cat, same maneuvers, same outcome. It became commonplace in my day to day.

One night I managed to find an interesting article about the White Cat that helped to answer why it was so dangerous to chase the harmless looking creature. I learned from this exceedingly detailed post that the cat is a trap—a failsafe program built into Y2 to seek out us "rogue programs." Once it discovers these defective programs, the White Cat is activated to lure them to a back door where they can be shut away. The author dubbed this prison of sorts "The Backrooms."

The same author wrote another excerpt explaining what he or she believed The Backrooms to be. It was referred to as more of a containment zone than a reprogramming station. From what I had gathered from reading, it seemed like a sinister place, though very little information was offered about what exactly it was. The articles from this author were dated for eight months ago…he or she hadn't written anything since then. Had he too fallen victim to the White Cat?

Armed with this information, I did well to continue to avoid the White Cat for as long as I could, but the persistent little beast kept impeding more and more into my life with each day that passed. The more I researched and read, the more intrusive the White Cat became to the point where I saw it roaming the building I worked in. One notable time I saw the infernal thing was when I went out to get some more coffee one Saturday morning, and at the end of the hall it sat. His pure white fur was such a stark contrast to the neutral grey of the walls and yellowish light that came from the nearby laundry room. It stood up and stared directly at me, then pranced about with its tiny claws clacking on the brown linoleum floor. I cautiously approached the cat, intending not to frighten it away. The feline slowly approached, sniffed at me, then rubbed across my ankles before flopping about at my feet in a playful manner. It was a cute fluffy thing with emerald eyes and a nose as pink as a strawberry candy. I'm not much of a cat person, but even I had to admit that this little thing was adorable.

When I knelt to pet it, my hand barely grazed the silken hairs of its coat before it scurried away to a corner. I watched as the little creature curled into a ball and yowled at me with eyes as big as dinner plates. I reached for it again, but it darted off into the stairwell. It turned to look at me one last time before I witnessed it disappear into wall. That's right, *into* a wall. The memory of the encounter stayed fresh in my mind for some time.

As I searched the web for more and more information about the White and The Backrooms, I came across a plethora of knowledge about the Year 2000 bug, also known as Y2. I found myself traveling down the rabbit hole about the inner and outer workings of the bug program that launched in the year 2000. Apparently, the program has shrouded reality in order to influence the day-to-day. No one knows for certain who was responsible for the bug's creation, just that it appeared at the most opportune moment. I had to admit to myself that there was something to this Y2K bug.

In the following weeks, I became introverted more than ever, alone in my internal battle for knowledge against the intricacies of the very structure that held us prisoner. I noticed more and more things I identified as "leaks" or "bad coding" in the system, such as the occurrence of déjà vu. For example, I was given the same greeting by the doorman who wore the exact same outfit: a red velour looking coat with a barely noticeable stain on his lapel, possibly from syrup. His black trousers were held up with a shiny black belt adorned with a glinting platinum buckle. His shoes were shined and, despite how straight he stood, his left foot always hooked slightly outward. He was the most apparent case of déjà vu: wearing that same stained jacket, the same pants, and always with the one hooked foot.

He'd open the door and say, "Morning Mr. Smith! Fine day, isn't it?"

I'd typically reply, "Beautiful day, indeed!" and proceed to thanking him for holding the door as I passed through it. I'd get in the elevator, press a button, and listen to an instrumental of Cheeseburger in Paradise on the way to my office's floor. It was the same thing every day; somehow, I had never paid enough attention to notice how unusual the usual was. The only things what would change in this routine was the weather. Perhaps that simplistic difference was enough to keep me ignorant.

Through my quests for knowledge, the White Cat was ever vigilant to the point where I welcomed seeing the little furball. The cat was the only thing I felt akin to, since no one else I knew personally was "awake" enough to understand what I had been going through. This damned cat became more of a companion to me, curling up near me and purring as if we were life-long friends. I was aware of the cat's ulterior motive, and that this kinship meant nothing at all, but I was so desperate for companionship that negated the truth in favor of imagining my own reality. The redundant days and reciprocating weeks wore my sharp mind down to a dull nub. When people reach their rock-bottom, they slip up and make mistakes. I'm not sure if it's because I created a Stockholm syndrome-like relationship with that feline per say, but, yes, obviously I slipped up because now I am in The Backrooms writing down my story with the pen I happened to have in my pocket on the day I entered the doorway atop paper scraps I've come across in my travels while here.

Unfortunately, I need to find more paper scraps so that I can continue my story. Look for my next entry where I will indulge you further with how I ended up here.

LETTER 2

The day it all went to shit started like any other day. I had no idea that my ground hog's day life was going to take a left turn at Albuquerque. I left my room, played with the cat until it fled and walked past the doorman who greeted me, as usual.

"Morning, Mr. Smith! Fine day, isn't it?"

Instead of following the routine, I stopped and stared at him, peering into his unblinking eyes. To my surprise, he wasn't put off by my stares. Instead, he stared through me as if I wasn't there and faintly smiled. It was as if he was waiting for the same greeting prompt, I typically gave ad nauseum.

"Beautiful day, indeed," I replied in a flat tone, still inches from his face. He stepped back, grasped the door, and opened it for me as he always had. He didn't seem perturbed by my odd behavior. Instead, he came off as an automation himself.

I went straight into the elevator with its mirrored walls and pressed the ivory-colored button for my floor: LL2. I rode along, hearing the same instrumental rendition of Cheeseburger in Paradise before the bell sounded for my floor.

The door slid open to reveal the White Cat sitting right outside it. I attempted again to pet it. Instead of allowing me to get close, it took off running. It was heading straight for the stairwell. In a split decision, I chased after it. I knew what this meant as I pursued the feline—I was letting myself fall victim to The Backrooms, but I no longer cared. I had had enough of the monotony of this way of life. I wanted definitive answers, and something different.

The doors to other rooms blinked past me in a blur of dark brown tones as I ran, but I wasn't fast enough. The cat squeezed its furry little behind into the cracked slit between the door and its frame. I burst through the door and caught a glimpse of it sprinting toward the basement. I kept in close pursuit of the cat, trying to keep just the proper distance as to not lose it but also not scare it into a speeding frenzy. I followed it until the cat vanished into a door that *originally* led to a maintenance room.

I had been down here a couple times, helping the hotel super with the internet network and other odds and ends, but it looked different than I remembered. This version of the door was thick and comprised of a highly lustrous metal-like chrome. Etched into its surface was message: Gateway External Storage 504

There was no going back. My thirst for knowledge outweighed rational thought. I pressed my palm on the door and closed my eyes. In the darkness of my eyelids, I witnessed a flash of white. When I opened my eyes again, I found myself here: The Backrooms.

I now wander the endless labyrinthian yellow hallways with countless rooms that make no geometrical or architectural sense. Rooms open up into other rooms of varying sizes, some no bigger than a walk-in closet. Most of these spaces, as I've come to discover, serve very little purpose.

I believe that this place is meant to break you. The low hum of the fluorescent lighting echoes against the surrounding dead silence. Every square inch permeates the smell of old musty carpet. I had hoped that over time my senses would become accustomed to the sights, smells, and sounds of The Backrooms, but so far everything is just as notable as the day I set foot in this place.

If that isn't enough, know that as you turn your back on your surroundings, they change on you. I thought I was going crazy at first until I realized that the rooms randomly blink in and out of existence in the blink of an eye. They generate arbitrarily to keep us lost, trapped. This makes charting a map a fruitless endeavor.

The only upside to this discovery is that the rooms containing objects never change out. This limitation to the system proves that these objects anchor the room in place. The permanent object can be anything: litter, clothing, scraps, droppings, etc. Because the object does not have a recognized code makeup within this realm, it cannot be replicated, and thus the room can no longer be mobilized and regenerated elsewhere. Could this be used to our advantage?

I don't have many tips that I can give you, unfortunately. All I can say is to do what's worked for me: keep your wits about you and, above all, keep moving. Sleep only when you need to. I will keep leaving letters behind in rooms for you and others to find. Hopefully my letters will act as an anchor for the room they land in. I will be able to provide better information in the future.

Keep moving, and may we find each other—Greg.

LETTER 3

I don't know if I will ever get used to this place. I hear the humming of the lights in my head. I try plugging my ears when going to sleep, but I hear that incessant noise despite my attempts.

Anyway, let me give you some advice to help you survive these Backrooms:

#1: Eat the soggy carpet pieces to stay satiated as well as hydrated but try not to think about *why* they are damp. There is some nutrition these soaked spots can offer, they've kept me going so far. I've also tried chiseling out pieces of the walls with the flat end of my pen—the walls are slightly more appetizing than the carpet, but not as filling. Still, what I wouldn't give for a proper meal. When I do dream, I've been having visions of food: cheeseburgers, pizza, chicken nuggets, hell even some vegetables squeezed in there. It doesn't help my hunger at all, but I try to envision the scraps I consume to be *real* food. Perhaps give that a try to help you get through the circumstances. My clothes barely fit and my stomach lurches at the thought of eating more of that damned carpet, but it's all we have.

#2: Leave behind what you can to mark a room as a constant. Write letters, like me, tear up and leave scraps of clothing, use rooms and halls as a bathroom, etc. I was fortunate enough to collect some more bits of paper as of late, so you may be lucky enough to find some too. I will also leave the back side of my pages blank for you to write on or use as you see fit. I will also assume that a writing instrument isn't in your possession. I suggest you find something thin and strong. I tried breaking a piece of molding off the wall and split it into shards. The "ink" I tried out were scrapes of mold accumulating around the wet spots on the floors.

#3: Find a way to maintain your sanity. Admittedly, the main reason for me writing these letters has been to preserve my mental stability more than communicating with you. Write if and when you can, it'll help keep your mind busy. Above all, we must try and keep our sanity. Once your mind starts slipping, you'll lose yourself. Believe me, I feel half dead as I write this.

Speaking of notes, I do have a bit of good news: I came across a bit of paper with some scribbling on it. This note was written with very legible handwriting, so I assume a woman wrote it. This person seems to have a firm grasp on programming and revealed more about The Backrooms in her note. The author alludes to the idea of this place having a back door line of code. This code spawns a very rare but recurring door that is rumored to be a way out. I don't know what the spawn rate of this door is, but this news gives me hope for a possible way out.

Finding this note also confirms to me that there are indeed other people in here. Up until this point, I had only suspected there were others. Now that I know you are out there, it changes things.

Since we inhabit a location sustained by code, it may be good to try some codes to see if they will run as they do on a computer, per say. I've been tinkering with code myself, so let me leave you my findings to try for yourself. I found that writing code on the walls will generate it into the space. For those of you better at coding than I am, you can use these basic codes as a steppingstone.

Here is one that I've tried: WHITE CAT: C:/directory/find/whitecat.run. It isn't much help, as it generates one of the white cat programs. The cat will appear and then immediately phase through the nearest wall. I originally thought that this prompt could help me find an exit, but it proved unhelpful. I tried to follow the program, but it was impossible with how the rooms randomly generate. Maybe you or someone else can find a better use for the code.

The other code I discovered was: GateGolden.exe. I found it written on a wall in what looked like blood. I haven't been able to find the proper prompt to put it in. So far, all my efforts have been fruitless. I know that isn't much help.

But we can't give up. All we can do is hope. We will find a way out of here. Just know that there IS an exit, there IS a way out.

Keep moving and we may find each other—Greg.

LETTER 4

I actually found someone! She's the one responsible for the scraps of coding. It was a woman, as I had suspected from the handwriting. Her name is…well, she told me to refer to her as Oleander. I don't think that's her real name, but maybe it was an alias she used? Not that it matters. What's important is that I found her!

Oleander is a red-headed firecracker with unbelievable intelligence. She said she's been in The Backrooms for a long time now and explained everything she knew about this place. She described The Backrooms to be like a prison of sorts for people that dug too deep into the Y2 program, which makes me wonder if she was the one that wrote the one article I had read, though I cannot remember the name of the author.

Speaking of Y2, she told me a bit more about it: Y2 is indeed an A.I. program meant to keep the clocks rolling after 1999 ended. The program was flawed, however, and failed to operate as expected. Instead of maintaining function, it became sentient, so to speak, and formulated a false reality.

Here comes the heavy part that I'm still trying to grasp myself: the world ended that night. When 1999 rolled into 2000, Y2 failed, causing nuclear fallout to ravage the globe and wipe out the entire populous in one apocalyptic sweep. But, when Y2 came up short, its backup files activated and wrote its own version of reality. It generated artificial consciousness and constructed life where there was none. The backup program succeeded, surpassing what was initially thought possible, which was why the transition was seamless to most after the downfall of humanity.

This then leads us all to the question: is it worth getting out of here to go back to what we now know isn't real? I don't know about you, but I still want to get back to that life. I may be aware of it, but it's better than being here. I'd rather die in a simulation than die in this yellow-tinged hellhole.

Oleander made a good point about this: being in The Backrooms is like getting a peek behind the curtain at the inner workings of our fabricated reality. She theorizes that returning to the simulation with this knowledge may endow us with the ability to alter our existence within the Y2 program. This means we could practically make ourselves gods, if we wish it. Wouldn't that be nice?

Oleander, just as she had mentioned in her note, theorizes that there is a way out through a certain door. Apparently, this door is to a "safe room." The only problem with this room is it is indistinguishable to every other door in The Backrooms. This "safe room," she believes, will have a back door that leads into the Y2 simulation. Unfortunately, Oleander has determined that the chance of any one of us finding this room is… one in a million and some odd change. Regardless of the odds being against us, it is still a glimmer of hope to strive for.

I'll keep writing until either my pen dries up or I run out of paper. So, while you're following my notes, take the time to check every room. If you find the room, then congratulations!

Keep moving, and we may find each other— Greg.

LETTER 5

I'm afraid I have some bad news: there are things out there meant to terminate us. I know this situation is already dire even without this new enemy, but, alas, nothing in The Backrooms is built in our favor. All I can hope is that this letter finds you before one of those things does. The "things" that I am referring to Oleander has dubbed "Minotaur."

Oleander and I came across one after we had settled in a room with an open doorway to rest. We managed to find a freshly soaked bit of carpet to feast upon, so we set up camp and ripped at the soggy rug. Oleander sat across from me and was scribbling what looked like vague coding and calculations on the wall behind her with a sharpened scrap of molding—an idea she got from me. Since my knowledge of code is limited, I can only hazard a guess as to what she was up to. I remained quiet and merely watched as she scribed her thoughts onto the wall. She always seems to be thinking over every little detail internally or through muttering to herself, which can't be healthy by any means for her—it certainly makes me feel uncomfortable if not inferior to her. It was like she preferred to seek council with herself over talking anything out with me. Perhaps she saw me as insignificant to her own brainpower too.

As Oleander was lost within herself, I heard a mechanical noise and a whirling sound unlike anything that I've heard before—very different from the buzzing of the lights. The sound was coming from beyond the doorway. It was getting louder, as if heading in our direction.

I turned to get Oleander's attention, but she too seemed to have become aware of the mechanical noise and put up a hand to keep me silent. Her eyes went wide in realization as the sound continued to grow louder. Oleander leapt at me, grabbing hold of my shirt and tugged at me to follow her to the far corner of the room we were in, away from the doorway to our room. We huddled together in silence as we watched the entrance. As the sound grew louder yet, Oleander began to shake in fear. What was it about these things that's got her so worked up?

Suddenly, the monstrosity made its way toward the doorway. My eyes nearly bugged out of my head at the sight of the sizable shadow cast upon the wall and floor beyond our room as it approached. Then, the nearly incomprehensible machine hovered past the doorway. A metal orb the size of a beach ball glided about four feet from the floor suspended within a dark grey metal shell. The shell was dotted with hundreds or purple tinted LED's. The "eye" of the machine, as Oleander referred to it, emanated a similar purple light that flickered within its center. The center was surrounded by several rotating rings backlit by this same light. The machine's hovering sound came from the odd motions of these rings as they rotated around the orb. Thankfully, it didn't spot us and kept on its way.

Oleander theorizes that the Minotaur patrol The Backrooms. She calls them Minotaur due to their resemblance to the creatures depicted in The Labyrinth. I don't find the connection as astute as she does, but I suppose giving them a name helps to make them slightly less ominous. I, on the hand, would like to find out if there is a way to stop them in order to harvest their parts. Perhaps there is some coding we could discover from one of their husks. Oleander thinks this is crazy, as she has no idea the capabilities of the Minotaur. She speculates that they must detain and delete those sentenced to the Backrooms… people like us.

I must admit it's a haunting idea: being deleted. Think about that. We don't know for certain where files go when deleted. Before this place, I would have imagined that a physical representation of The Backrooms would be the destination for deleted programs. But if we occupy these Backrooms, then where would we go if deleted? I shudder to think of what deletion means in this context.

Since we don't know much about the Minotaur, we have very little knowledge on how to combat them. I'm not sure you even can, to be honest. The only thing I know to do is to duck into the nearest room and hide. Try and stay out of eyeshot if possible. If you hear one coming, stay calm and don't run. This would draw unwanted attention to yourself and could possibly give away your hiding spot.

Another theory Oleander and I have been tooling with is that some of the rooms are a stationary constant, and not due to having objects in them. I swear I've seen the same couple of rooms in the same place regardless of random generation. Our theory to legitimize this phenomenon is "hashtag pockets." In programming, hashtag coding is used as a cheat of sorts so that a portion of the main code can be recalled so the programmer doesn't have to keep writing out the same lines of code over and over again. We think these stationary rooms are sanctioned by hashtag commands. I believe that there are a variety of hashtag rooms, perhaps hundreds, that will always stay in the same place. These areas may come in handy somehow.

I know things look more and more grim, but we must try and stay focused. Stay focused on the endgame.

Keep moving and may we find each other –
Greg.

LETTER 6

I've been finding myself seeing things in my peripheral that Oleander isn't seeing. I worry that I am losing my mind. I worry that the longer we go on like this, the less likely we are to escape.

Oleander keeps insisting that there is a door. I have to admit that her persistence makes the idea seem possible, but to what end? What if she is going crazy too? What if this door plan is her slip into madness? I'll never know, unfortunately. What I do know is that I can't really trust her anymore—when we lay down to sleep, I find myself keeping a semi-vigilant eye on her. This, of course, has affected my sleep even more than listening for the Minotaur.

Then again, without her I don't know how long I would survive… so, there is the other caveat. Had it not been for her warning about the Minotaur, I more than likely would have stumbled into and fallen victim to one.

Speaking of falling victim, despite feeling as though I cannot trust her, I feel attached to Oleander. It may be one-sided, but I've taken to imagining that she and I are a young married couple still getting to know and love one another. I go out of my way to treat Oleander well and try to do nice things for her, like offer her the larger pieces of damp carpet or the larger wall shavings I've collected. It's all pretend, of course, much like with the White Cat (if you had read that previous entry), so I don't think it's going to hurt anyone. At the most, it has helped to keep my mind busy.

Do you remember when you were a kid and played cops and robbers? You'd have nothing but your imagination, but the gun and uniform would feel real, as was the heist or shootout you were acting out. In those moments you'd forget about all your worries; the bully at school, bad grades, or anything that weighed heavy on your mind. This is why I'm pretending with Oleander; it's my coping mechanism. I'm trying to forget how heavy our situation is.

I hope you find something that helps you. Shit, I hope you've found your way out of here already and all I'm doing is writing letters to a ghost.

… a ghost…

That gives me an idea! It's funny how things can pop into your head randomly. This is going to sound crazy but try and follow my logic on this. I'm not sure if you're familiar with the idea of "no-clipping, so let me explain." Since this place is nothing more than a program, no-clipping would allow us to travel out of its boundaries. This would allow us to go beyond the halls and see everything from the vacuous space outside of its programming. With this idea in mind, we may even be able to find this door that Oleander keeps going on about.

The issue with this theory is that the space and boundaries of The Backrooms are unknown. We have no way of knowing what out-of-bounds looks like or how to navigate it. The boundaries very well could be an endless sea of Backrooms. Much like that of a repeating number, such as Pi, there could be endless rooms appearing and disappearing to the edge of space. This could make it impossible to navigate.

The other concern about no-clip is how to go about activating it. No human could activate a no-clip command. But, what if we aren't human like we thought. Are we stuck here because we are adhering to humanity's rules? Does thinking of this place as a physical series of hallways and rooms enslave us to its form? Would using mathematics change it to our will?

This then leads me to the next paradox: say we escape and go back to our respective realities, what's to say that Y2 hadn't already replaced us to keep others ignorant? There is a possibility of that. If we have been replaced, could returning corrupt or crash Y2? The sudden shock of generating so many lines of repeating code, or code that was once deleted, could cause the system to glitch or fail, possibly destroying everything we know. Is it worth the risk?

For now, I can only test my theory and hope to God that I don't bring the house of cards tumbling down.

Keep moving, and we may find each other—Greg.

LETTER 7

To whomever has been reading the letters that Greg has left behind, I'm afraid I have bad news for you: Greg is dead. I don't really know how else to break it to you than to be frank about it. So, yes, Greg passed away a short while ago.

He was insistent about his theory regarding no-clipping, and how it had to be our way out of here. Sadly, he wasn't sure how to execute it. He debated so much on the matter that it was almost maddening. He proclaimed that the only way to get no-clipping to work was to overload his mind to the point where his newfound perception of reality superseded his belief of reality. I, for one, am unsure that his idea is even possible, but no matter how much I tried to talk Greg down, he persisted. His attempts to activate no-clipping, of course, didn't work. He tried to phase through the walls by slamming into them again and again. I don't want to go into gruesome detail over Greg's demise, but do not do this.

I have no answers as to how to perform an actual no-clip, but I can certainly tell you that Greg's theory isn't the way, as it will result in death. If that's your course of action, however, I cannot stop you.

If you are as fervent as I to escape this place, then we should try to work together. Greg may have referred to me as Oleander in his letters, so I'll continue to refer to myself as such. My actual name is of no importance anymore.

I will honor Greg's death by continuing to write letters. I feel that, if I find a way out, I owe it to you to pass on my knowledge. If there is a key, and I believe there is, I will detail any thoughts, ideas, or coding that I discover along the way. Journaling my efforts won't be a burden, as Greg and I had made a habit of collecting plenty of scrap papers and materials. I have what I need, for now, to carry on in Greg's stead.

Much like Greg, I too have a hypothesis on getting out of here, but, unlike his, it requires less physical assault. I fully believe that a back door exists, since every program has one. We just need to find a way to locate it. I believe the Minotaur machines are the key. They must enter and exit The Backrooms via some sort of door. The only problem we face is trying to track them without being seen.

I plan on honoring Greg, by giving him some kind of funeral. We may be facsimiles of our old selves, but the ideals of our humanity remain.

If it helps, stranger, remember Greg's words:

Keep moving, and we may find each other.

—Oleander

LETTER 8

It occurred to me the other day that Greg's idea just might hold water. To put it bluntly, however, I don't indorse you trying to phase through the walls. We both know what that will get you. Of all the things to clue me in on this notion, it had to be a Minotaur. I heard the signature whirling noise as it neared my hiding place.

I noticed in one of Greg's letters that he mentioned stationary rooms using a hashtag protocol. This does happen, but he incorrectly informed you about the characteristic they share: they always have litter in them. The randomly generated rooms are usually clean as whatever matter/data in them is phased out of existence. By my calculations, the hallways and rooms seem to regenerate rather slowly.

I managed to follow one of the Minotaur and discovered that they can no-clip! As trailed it, I saw it happen right before my eyes—the machine turned and headed straight into a wall. Once phased into the wall, the sound it was making ceased. This must be how they travel around. At first, I felt devastated by this discovery because it put a hole in my door theory. But, it did prove that no-clipping is possible.

Now, before we go jumping for joy over this breakthrough, we must take into account that there is more than likely something in their programming that allows them to do this. I still can't wrap my brain around how this trick is done. Hopefully, one pf us can figure it out.

For what it is worth, these letters are serving a purpose to not only give me an outlet but also pass on what I know to you.

Keep going. Please find me – Oleander

LETTER 9

This place has made me ponder the concept of death. Before coming here, I thought of death as a natural process—the final journey awaiting us, as I'm sure you did as well. It's a constant; something that is even more cemented in our existence than anything else. To be frank, death is guaranteed, whereas most other things are trivial. That was the way it worked before, when our mortal coils weren't comprised of lines of code.

The thought of life and death being compressed down into numbers takes the majestic nature out of it. I've found myself wondering if death and life, in the simulation, is simplified down to a simple RNG process. I believe this is the case.

This makes me wonder if life is still life when it's artificially generated and governed by a program straight out of dystopian fiction. I suppose that is up to the individual, to some degree. I find it ironic that we, the rogue programs, have more freedom to make that decision versus those within the simulation who are ignorant to the lie they live. Is that luck? I really cannot say. We are at the disadvantage of having to fight to get back to that lie, or the advantage of giving it up.

Could you imagine what things would be like if those in the simulation were "awake" like us? I don't think many would continue for long until they ended their lives or fought the system looking for freedom, like we did.

I realize that this all seems like rambling. I figure that it would only be fair to voice this epiphany in case you didn't think of it yourself. We are more human here than in the network. Take the time now to decide for yourself if you want to trade free will for a fake life. Personally, I'll take the fake life regardless of it being another form of prison.

If you decide to continue, as I do, keep going, please find me – Oleander

LETTER 10

This marks the tenth letter corresponding between Greg and I. When I first ran into Greg, or more precisely, he into I, he went on and on about how he was leaving letters. He thought of them as a breadcrumb trail through the forest. Indeed, the idea is a valiant one, though possibly misdirected, I fear. They blip out with the rooms; they do not stay like Greg had hoped.

I am not typically very fond of humans, though I did try to coexist with them. I often thought of them as the bane of our planet, when we had one. Like water off a duck's ass, I'd try to let the little imperfections of our kind roll off my back. From time to time, I'd find myself conversing with some people that are an exception to that rule. Greg was one such individual. The time he wasted writing out these letters or having me painstakingly reiterate my findings so that he could dumb it down was infuriating, yes, but also kind. He could have worried about himself, but he didn't. I miss him now. I came to trust him. If we had found a way out of here together, we'd more than likely be life-long friends. He was a light in the darkness that sadly burned out before it should have. It made me realize the frailty of our existence.

Existence. That's a word I've been using a lot of as late. I suppose I find it somewhat charming as the ideal of the word itself is rather moot now. Is it truly "existing" when your mind is open to the realization that you're nothing more than code? When everything is predetermined, is that truly "existing?" I suppose it is one way to exist, depending on your values, goals, and dreams.

Speaking of dreams, that is another enigma I've been pondering over. I'm not sure about you, but I still dream in this place. This confuses me, as dreams, I as thought them to be, were collections of subconscious thoughts or worries distilled down into nonsensical visions. I don't know how a machine would project dreams, or even if it was possible for it to do so. But, when you think about what the "real world" is currently, is that nothing but a dream? Are simulations simply dreams?

I want to leave you with something helpful. I stumbled upon an anomaly within The Backrooms recently: I turned a corner and found a hallway unlike any other. The hall was impressively long and was lined with doors on each side. Above the head of each door sat a line of binary code. The code is all white in digital font face and flickers like a holographic projection.

In case you're not familiar with binary, it's a simple coding method for words/commands that are comprised of sequences of ones and zeros. Example: 00 01 11 10. Noticing this above the doors piqued my interest as I am fairly familiar with that style of coding. I studied a few of the doors and managed to decipher some of their titles. One door was labeled CONTRAST, while the one directly across from it was ARRIVAL. The fact that any of these codes represent actual words is a miracle in itself. For the first time in God knows how long, I feel like I am making progress.

The hall also seems to be a constant. I watched it, witnessing the rooms outside of the hall transform anew, but this hall remained. I don't know how versed you are in coding, but if this is what I think it is, I may have stumbled upon another crucial instrument for our escape. This corridor could be a master line of code in The Backrooms programming. I'm not sure how much you know about coding, but a master line works similar to hashtag codes. This master line of code gets called back to when a program is generating a similar code in order to get the framework right. Think of it as an echo; you shout, then the sound reverberates to repeat what you shouted. Except, in this case, the code is replicated perfectly and then augmented to fit as needed for the code's new makeup. Since this hallway is still here and binary over the doors remains unchanged, I wholeheartedly believe this to be a master code.

At this time, I do not understand its purpose, but I plan to investigate it further. I intend to stay here to learn more. If I am right, this discovery could change everything.

I will continue writing you letters when I can. I have amassed so much litter to write on that I could write a book, so no worries there.

The only issue I must solve is sustenance. The hall is not carpeted. So, perhaps I will need to dip into one of the changing rooms to grab nourishment from time to time.

That being said, I will be leaving all further letters at either end of the hall, alternating sides with each entry. If you find any titled ten or higher, you may be close to me. I would suggest staying close to the respected area. You never know what you could stumble upon turning a corner.

I will also leave you a list of the rooms I've deciphered thus far. There are dozens more for me to translate, but here are the current lot:

- CONTRAST
- ARRIVAL
- EGGSHELL
- TRAVELER

That is all I have. Keep moving. Please find me—Oleander

LETTER 11

I believe the words I deciphered are indeed parts of a programming code for The Backrooms. They all mean something! They have to! With each break in the code, I feel like I'm getting close to figuring out their purpose. Harkening back to my C+ programming days in high school, the same ideas apply to most coding. Most OS programming, even current day Windows, can be accessed using command prompts, much like DOS. However, DOS is the manual method. Today, most codes run automatically and seamlessly without the need to open the command prompt window.

I think the phrases that I've stumbled upon are keywords to insert into RUN: prompts. The only thing I can't figure out is the exact coding line they need to be placed into to successfully execute their RUN directive. I will have to think about this some more in order to discover a solution. Afterall, we are all technically run prompts. Our actions within this place do have an effect; we can leave behind remnants of ourselves, eat from the walls and floor, and even die in here, like a running code until it is deleted.

Also, as I mentioned in a previous letter, Greg was onto something with his no-clipping theory and reaching beyond our mental limitations of what we are. We keep thinking that we are physical beings in the sense of flesh and bone. Even I am guilty of this. But, alas, we are program codes; our codes must, at the very least, coexist within the infostructure of this program in order for it to be a punishment or a storage space for "rogue programs" like us.

There is still plenty of fine tuning to work out, but I have a hypothesis regarding how to perform an access command. If I am right, it may be our ticket out of here. If not, then it's back to the drawing board. Write this down on any of the letters you find or have found. If my theory works, the letters you write this on should end up back in this hallway:

DIRECTORY A/: RUN: COMMAND - HALL/DIRECTORY. EXE

If you're more versed in coding than I am, perhaps you'd be able to work with this idea and fix the code to execute it better. Again, this is only a theory, but I feel like I have an edge with this. If this code works, it may blow the lid off navigating around The Backrooms. It's worth a shot anyway.

Keep moving. Find me—Oleander

LETTER 12

I discovered something today that is both exciting and troubling. I spent some time studying more of the doors and deciphered one that had my name on it: OLEANDER. Now, you may be aware that Oleander isn't my real name, but I find it to be too much of a coincidence that this word would show up on one of these doors. What are the chances? I haven't come across another door labeled with anything close to a person's name until this point.

I'm tempted to go in the door to discover its secrets, though I am concerned that it could be a trap. I would like to think that Y2 is bound by the normal laws of programming; ergo, everything will have a coinciding file to document it. Then there is the other side of the coin. The program's sole purpose is to lie to us, so what would make me think that it wouldn't do things such as this to trap us? The Backrooms were meant as a jail of sorts anyway and we are meant to die in here.

That brings me to another strange occurrence. Since I've found this hallway, I haven't heard any Minotaur approach. You'd think that would bring me some reprieve, but it honestly bothers me. What is it with this hallway that keeps them at bay? Did I wander into a part of the programming that not even Y2 thought a person could find? I think it unlikely, but I can't help but consider that possibility.

The Backrooms and Y2 govern everything. Before I found this hallway, I hadn't a moment's worry that I was losing my mind. Now that I'm getting close to something, I'm having these thoughts, much like Greg did. It could be a failsafe, to keep us from escaping. I just hope that I can find a way around it and keep my mind clear.

Earlier, I did mention the codes I figured out. Here they are:

- AMBER
- CONTACT
- BETA
- SENTRY
- RUN
- GLASS
- VAULT
- OLEANDER
- GENERATE
- CITY

I also want to rewrite the code from the previous letter. The more letters I include it on, the more likely you are to find it: DIRECTORY A/: RUN: COMMAND - HALL/DIRECTORY. EXE

If you have nothing to write with, try rubbing it onto a wall with garbage, blood, or filth. I'd even try scratching it into something soft… like skin perhaps?

If any of this works, you may be able to work outside the program and get The Backrooms to work in your favor. Also, try switching the word HALL with any of the keywords I listed earlier, excluding my name. If you have other ideas on how to work activating the codes, please do so. Any sort of breakthrough will be a win. Nothing is impossible.

Impossible. That word has resonated with me more as of late. I find myself being very thankful for the impossible things I have achieved so far, though they were attained out of complete happenstance. My programming knowledge hasn't helped much so far. The thing about the word impossible is it contains the word possible. I am inside of a construct that is all but impossible to navigate, yet I've found it possible to move on. Even in utter darkness there is light. Each moment can bring a breakthrough. Each thought can breed a theory worth trying. Impossibilities are the foundation of possibilities. I will not be held back by thinking anything is impossible.

I'm going to be honest, if I find a way out, I will not wait for you. I expect the same from you; do whatever you need to do to get yourself out of here. I know in other letters I begged you to find me mostly because I've been hating the solitude as of late, but I can't ask you to wait me for me. If you've cracked a code and have a gateway out, then take it!

Keep moving. Try to escape—Oleander.

LETTER 13

I did it…I went inside the door…but I am unsure of what I discovered.

d. It all felt like a dream, like the ghostly apparition of a memory. The grandeur of the room was far more than I could comprehend, among its contents. I'm sorry, I realize that I'm babbling—allow me a moment to collect my thoughts.

After I wrote the last letter, I went to send it off into one of the rooms at the end of the hall. As I released it into a room, I watched it dampen slightly from a patch of soaked carpet. I felt my mouth water at the sight of liquid wetting the page from the soggy flooring it sat upon. Who knew that one could miss moldy carpet as sustenance. Eventually, the letter, as well as the room I placed it in, blinked away and a new space emerged, then I returned to my little camp outside the door with my name. I listened to the all too familiar sound of the lights humming overhead and thought about how I barely noticed the noise anymore. I had all but become deaf to the humming lights. It's funny how adaptable humans can be, isn't it? We can tune out stimulus to a point where it almost seems as if it is no longer present.

I thought about what it might be like to finally leave The Backrooms for whatever resided on the other side of that illusive exit door I've talked about before. It's funny, but the very thought of leaving this place stirred feelings of sadness and loss within me.

Being here almost felt homely now, given how long I have been here. If I was to be examined by a shrink, I'm sure Stockholm Syndrome would be the diagnosis. I've compared my symptoms to those of inmates who've done their time in jail, then are finally set free. The world they knew was gone. Finding that new path in a world they no longer understood seemed daunting. Most don't make it. If I were to sum my feelings up in that moment into one word, it would be "bittersweet."

I waited and waited for you to show up, but nothing came of it. Truthfully, I was hoping someone would appear so that I wouldn't have to face the door alone. I'm desperate for someone to be here with me, like Greg was. He helped to keep me grounded. Without him, I find my mind slipping in all directions. If someone came here, that would help me once again stay grounded. What we could gain from working together would be so much better than being alone, not only for me, but also for you, I'm sure.

Still, how long would it be until you meet the same fate as Greg? Would I have to watch you snap too? I had to watch him degrade into insanity. I'm not sure I could handle that again. So, perhaps it was better I was alone for my venture beyond my door.

After delaying for as long as I had, I finally approached the door. I placed a hand upon its white glossy veneer; it felt cold and slick like glass. The coding at the head of the door illuminated a brighter white as a slit manifested at waist height upon the door. A silver handle protruded from the slit. The opening closed around the handle, anchoring it into place with a loud click. The coding above the door then dimmed to its original level of light. The exterior of the door suddenly cascaded with binary—a sequence of 1's and 0's. The falling text was hypnotic, like watching rain trickling down a window. As the sequence ended seconds later, the door vanished, and I was greeted with a flash of white light.

I peered through the open doorway to the vast white space beyond it filled with plumes of hazy fog. There was very little I could see from where I was, so I entered the room, stepping upon a well-polished dark metal disc emanating a haunting red glow from beneath. The disc began moving once my full weight was upon it. It traveled straight into the room, not deviating in either direction. Around me I could not make heads nor tails of any landmarks. The whiteout shrouded anything that could have been lurking in the distance.

After some time of being ushered along, I caught sight of what looked like a portal in the distance. The perimeter of the portal was adorned with metal shards comprised of a similar metal to the disc. These shards entangled around one another like bramble, their thorns jutting wildly in all directions.

My platform drew closer, eventually stopping about twenty feet away. I wasn't sure what to do at first. I feared plummeting to my death, but I realized when I looked down that I was not hovering over a white void as I had originally thought. The floor beneath me was glass encasing a less impervious cloud cover that shrouded a sprawling mountain range of hexagonal stone totems. Their tops were flattened and scribed with a symbol carved into each peak. These pillars stretched on into the vista beyond, seemingly going on for infinity. Below my platform, among the valley of stone columns, was a seal. This seal looked to be the same size as the portal with the binary code. My name was carved into its surface in binary code.

The numeric code on the seal irradiated with the same red glow that my disc had. I watched as a slit in its face opened and a shard of dark metal emerged. The sliver floated up toward me. A panel in the glass floor opened and allowed the fragment to pass through. It hovered before me as a red glyph in the shape of a tree lit up on its face. I instinctively touched the glyph which caused a shot of blue light to spark down to the valley below. The light snaked through the pillars, illuminating each peak as it powered the portal before me.

I held my breath, bracing for the next sequence to happen. My eyes were fixated on the portal as it emanated a faint blue glow from its center. The light between the mountainous columns traveled up a massive metal shaft that rose to the base of the conduit. The metal shards surrounding the portal started to spin, emanating a series of shrill clangs as they cycled around the gateway. The metal ring spun faster and faster, their details vanishing behind their blurring speed. Their increasing velocity caused a deep hum to fill the room as the portal sparked to life with a cyclone of cobalt light.

In that moment I smelled something odd, yet familiar. It reminded me of the slight burning scent of old oil. The stale smell took my mind back to my childhood, making me think of Christmas and the gentle glow of the warm white lights on my tree and the smell coming from the old candles that burned in each window.

The triggered memory made me wonder even more about how efficient Y2's programming was. Was that memory organic or simply something cued up in my data? It got me thinking of a programming term called culling. Simply put, culling is used to keep things out of reach or sight until they are absolutely either meant to be seen or put into queue. Culling also works in programming code as well. Much like a hashtag, culling a line of code keeps it in line and ready to be called back to. It's always there but ignored unless otherwise needed to complete a sequence. Think about it simply like this: you can't see behind you unless you turn around or use a mirror. It's culled out until it needs to be there to support a demand, like a surface to walk on or something to be seen.

This same principle works for the hallways in The Backrooms as well. The difference with the rooms, of course, are that they are randomly being culled in and out in order to maintain a maze-like structure. I believe this portal that I found works within the same principle; it's always here, but it needs to be powered up in order to work.

The disk I was perched upon was drawn toward the gateway. There was a ten foot gap between the portal and me. As the conduit hummed and the light within swirled with greater intensity, shards of glass emerged from the white abyss below me and connected to one another. The shards formed a bridge that spanned the gap between me and the gate.

I cautiously placed a foot upon the glass. It was thin and felt fragile, but thankfully supported my weight. I continued, walking forward as gingerly as I could, hoping that this wasn't an elaborate trap.

After a couple more cautious strides I stood before the gate. The following occurrence was a blur. I honestly don't know what happened, but as I waited before the gate, I felt dizzy, then the next thing I knew I was in a completely different room and the portal was behind me.

This room was also white and vast, though the walls were visible on each side. The ceiling was a cavernous void while the walls and floor were comprised of a lustrous white tile. The only other thing of note within this space was a gargantuan dark metal orb that levitated in the center.

The orb was segmented into several jutting panels that encased a red glowing center. The panels floating around the red glowing center were spaced slightly apart to allow the light to shine between them. The light inside the orb pulsated several times as I stared at it, then it let out a blinding red flash. I blinked hard to readjust my eyes and discovered a change in the room after the burst of light: three more portals had appeared upon the previously barren walls of the room.

This room piqued my curiosity; what could all of these gateways mean? I decided to investigate. I walked the circumference of the room, studying each conduit in turn, measuring the similarities as well as their differences. At the apex of each portal sat a panel with a symbol, much like the ones I saw engraved on the pillars in the previous room. Each symbol resembled something I was familiar with, yet it was unlike anything I had ever seen before.

Although I was curious, I dared not activate any of the portals. This room felt malicious. I wasn't sure if it was the glowing red hues and alien-like dark metal objects, but I couldn't bring myself to venture further. There was no telling where one of these conduits could bring me. I could be freed, or end up in a Minotaur factory, or in some endless snowy-white purgatory. I felt that I had explored enough for this trip. It was time to head back to the safety of the hall.

I turned back and fled through the portal that brought me to this room. I was thankful to discover that the gates returned me to where they had brought me—meaning I was able to get back to the hall the same way I had left it. The metal platform brought me back to the door that led back into the hallway.

Everything worked the same in reverse, much to my relief.

I had half expected to lose the hallway and be trapped wandering these white corridors forever. Even now with how far I had gotten, everything still feels like a trap. I hate that there is no sense of safety anywhere, not even in the hall. I thought that once I vacated The Backrooms that I'd have this huge stress lifted from me, but the future seems even more bleak.

My hands are shaking as I write this letter. My mind is reeling with possibilities, each more unsettling than the last, and accompanied by a sense of dread. I can't help but worry that I'm playing right into Y2's hands. This could all be a pre-programmed series of events and I'm the mouse being led to the poisoned cheese. On the other hand, I must acknowledge the Schrodinger's cat thesis. I cannot confirm nor deny what dwells on the other side of those portals; I can only assume the best or worst. But until I go through with it, my assumption is that the cat is dead on the other side of those spaces.

01001111011011000110010101100001011011 01100110010001100101011100010

That is my name in binary code. I don't care how you use it: write it on the walls, on the bottom of letters, on trash or what have you. There has to be a way to reroute things back to me here. If this plan works, then we can start thinking of how to move people instead of simply objects to my location.

Keep moving. Find me—Oleander

LETTER 14

I had a close call. I was inspecting the hallway, going over more code, when I heard a sound that made my heart sink. The whirling hum of a Minotaur echoed through the corridors beyond the hall, though it was still out of sight. My stomach lurched as the noise drew closer. My hands convulsed in fear, their shivers radiated up my forearms and clutched at my neck. I felt the uncontrollable urge to hyperventilate as my mind ran wild with the possibilities of being caught.

As the noise grew louder, and the smell of burning oil crept through the halls, my hope faded into leeching anxiety. My legs felt wobbly as the sensation of static electricity flicked through the finer hairs on my body, making them stand on edge as one of those machines rounded the corner of the hall.

I have no idea if the Minotaur can travel into the doorways. Their coding is still such a mystery to me. I had seen them phase through walls once before, which makes me uncertain if there are restrictions on that trait. Can it only be exploited in The Backrooms? Or can it also be used in the white rooms?

The Minotaur hung there at the end of the hall, the purple light in its center eye shifted into a magenta tone. The machine let out a series of odd noises I could only equate to the sounds an old dot matrix printer makes. I was unsure what it was doing, but I assumed it couldn't be good.

Suddenly, from the other end of the hall, I heard another whirring sound. I nearly froze, but my morbid curiosity won over reason. I turned to spot yet another Minotaur. It too emanated the old printer-like noises as it turned and hovered at the entryway. They had me boxed in.

Despite having me cornered, neither Minotaur entered the hall. You would think this would put me at ease, but it makes this situation more threatening—like I'm being monitored. As I write this letter, they are seemingly studying me—they follow my movements, every now and then producing those odd sounds as if they are processing something. I can only assume that I am being watched…by what or whom is the big question.

I had more I wanted to talk about, but I should probably end it here and see how I can get this letter sent out to you. I also need to keep as close an eye on the Minotaur as they are of me. For now, they are staying put. As long as they don't cross the edge of the hall, I will continue my work.

Keep moving. Find your way out —Oleander.

LETTER 15

I'm stuck here, it seems, as they watch over me, forcing me to listen to the irritating processing noise coupled with the hum of their floating bodies. I never imagined that the Minotaur were little more than hall monitors. I thought they were capable of killing or sending the programs they find wherever it is programs go when they're deleted.

It's a funny and yet macabre thing to think about: what happens when a program…like you and I…is deleted. A human life, or what we now presume to be a human life, ending without much of a trace, as a program would in a computer system, is disheartening. We think of ourselves and our little world as the pinnacle of intelligent life, but in the end, we can all be replaced in the blink of an eye by a machine.

If my flesh and bones are nothing more than lines of code or numbers, am I really human? I don't know how to respond to that question, really. I feel pain, sadness, anger, joy, love…is that all not real? I don't believe things like that can be faked by computers. I have free will, which arguably is a human trait. I chose the path that led me to my current predicament—following the damned White Cat, for example. Curiosity, another human trait, causes us to question instinct or probability in favor of exercising free will. A soul, another arguably human trait, may also be something that cannot be replicated by a computer. So, can a soul stay attached to us if we are made of code? Does that mean that the soul can exercise free will as well and choose its vessel? If so, that may render the vessel no longer important.

In theory then, our souls transitioned to our data counterpart when our physical bodies ceased to be on the night that Y2K happened. I have no proof of this other than me being me and you being you—the same me and you that existed before Y2 activated. My body might not be what it once was, but my soul is still the same. In that case, we can deduce that the vessel is not what's important—it is our soul, our free will, and our curiosity that make us who we are.

This level of realization has admittedly brought me to tears. It is as if I have broken a chain tethering me to this horrible place and am that much closer to freedom. I do hope that this revelation has moved you in a similar way.

The fact that I have had no interaction with you or anyone else so far means either no one has received my letter, or the coding you've tried has not worked. That's fine. I'm willing to wait for you, if it means I can avoid leaving my hallway haven for a bit longer. I'm not looking forward to going through my door just yet, especially alone.

I've been killing time by writing these letters as well as deciphering some more binary codes I've seen within the cracks of these doors and upon the walls of the hallway. These codes seem to show up quite often, as some of them are also above some of the doors in my hall:

EGGSHELL -
01000101011001110110011101110011011010000011
001010110110001101100

CONTRAST -
0110001101101111011011011100111010001110010011
0000101110011011110100

GLASS -
0110011101101101100011000010111001101101110011

VAULT -
0101011001100001011101010110110001110100

METAL -
0100110101100101011010001100001011011 00

ARRIVAL -
010000010111001001110010011010010111011001 1
0000101101100

TRAVELER -
0101010001110010011000010111011001100101011
01100011001010111 0010

There isn't more I can say right now, unfortunately. I am running out of configurations to decipher. I'm still not sure you should even try to use them, since the Minotaur are still watching. I can only advise that you maybe just try sending me a letter back here, not try sending yourself, until we know for sure you will make it here safely.

I implore you to take a moment to cherish yourself before moving forward – Oleander.

LETTER 16

After much consideration, I've decided that I will return to my room without you. I can't risk sitting here much longer. The Minotaur aren't leaving, I'm hungry and exhausted, and there is nothing left to decipher. This hallway was a comfortable place, in contrast to beyond that door. The white void beyond the door seems unfit for human survival. Navigating it is another trepidation; I fear the consequences should I choose a wrong portal or do something incorrectly.

The other worry I have is the transmission of these letters. I have no guarantee any of them will be sent out. The "Oleander" room doesn't act like The Backrooms do; nothing inside that white void is randomly generated. Because of this, I will have to do some tinkering to expedite the letters in a different manner, maybe by rerouting them to the other rooms inside the hallway. Here are the codes I plan to use:

DIRECTORY A/: RUN: COMMAND - #HALL/ #VAULT / EXPIDITE. EXE

DIRECTORY A/: RUN: COMMAND - #VAULT ARCHIVES/ EXPIDITE .EXE

DIRECTORY A/: RUN: COMMAND - #BACK_ROOMS/ EXPIDITE.EXE

I will only use these codes on letters.

It is up to you whether you try to use these codes on letters as well, or for personal travel, as I would imagine once I leave, the Minotaur will move on. I personally do not know how to conduct using the codes for personal travel, other than possibly writing the code on your skin, theoretically. These commands, if written on the walls, might guide a room in The Backrooms to the hallway I was in.

Also, a side note and a refresher on a binary coding:

0100111101101100011001010110000101101 110011001000110010101110010

This is the binary code of my room. Look for this sequence if you decide to expedite any of the above commands and are successful. We may never meet, but you are welcome to try it.

One final note of thought: the amount of variables The Backrooms has in it appears like an infinite amount, but I feel that is an illusion. Even the world's most prodigious computers have a finite amount of disk space. An operating system working at such a capacity would definitely get bogged down. I think most of The Backrooms is comprised of several duplicated rooms and hall configurations that are shuffled and placed in different sequences. This would lighten the load on computing space and allow it to run without lag or error.

How do we use this to our advantage? This question has been bouncing around in my head. I'm really not that sure, but anything that shows a crack in the veneer will help us. Maybe running too many codes created by us will cause a system crash and with it a reboot? The next worry is, what will that do to us? Food for thought I suppose.

Keep moving—Oleander

LETTER 17

I'm starting to doubt who I really am and what this is all about. I keep telling myself to move forward, but there is one solitary thought that stabs at me like an ice pick: "What's the point?" It wasn't until now that I fully grasped the meaning of the question.

What's the point? Really, what is the point? I mean, we get out of here, and then what? It seems fitting that the only way out of this is to become comfortable with the notion of being a cog in the machine when we return to our world. I used to think living in a simulation like where we were was the worst scenario. Now, I'm dying to get back to it. Is that really worth all of this trepidation? Is giving away my free will a fair trade for a more acute version of freedom? I really don't know if I have a real answer to that question.

What is freedom anyway? Is it being able to have all your memories from before Y2's initiation? Do you remember being younger? Do you remember your first love, or even the first time you liked someone so much you wanted to tell them, but you weren't sure you could? Do you remember your first summer? The first day of school? Having those memories is all we have from our past lives. They are the scraps that remain of what we once were before a program took over and generated what it assumed our lives would be.

My hubris was not knowing when to stop searching for answers. I assumed I was far too intelligent to fall for any traps. I laughed off the warning to not follow the White Cat. There were so many warning signs, yet I found myself sprinting for that finish line.

Even now, I sit here battling internally for self-care and atonement as my brain is still quarreling with my heart—I still hunger for more information. Despite the downward spiral, I must find solace somehow with this paradox. Maybe I never will, but at this point, I feel like I owe it to myself to learn what I can and fuel a revolution for us. My progress could be the key to ridding the system of this unjust and hellish purgatory.

What is it about us that no matter the circumstance, we humans will strive to have a semblance of life that we deem "normal?" No matter what, even if we are told it is bad for us, we won't stop until we get that normality back? But why? Just so we can continue on with the familiar and mundane. Or, is it more that "change" is the true enemy? I really can't say, nor can I blame people for wanting life to be the same. I know what is out there; I know it is all a fake, but I want it back. I want it back because this version of life is not meant for humans, or rogue programs, or whatever it is we truly are. Perhaps, I miss the high I could get from excelling at my boring predictable life, whereas in this place everything is a threat. Maybe I am addicted to the very thing I once so desperately tried to escape from: normality. If there is a chance for survival, I'd be a dolt not to try.

For that reason, I decided to go through with my plan. I am not certain if these letters will find you anymore, but I will continue to send them. It creates a tether between us and helps keep me sane. Even if you're not real, and a part of the fictitious world I am trapped in, I feel like I have someone to talk to, and that feels like a slice of home.

Besides these letters, I have one other weapon in my arsenal to keep me sane: my friends and family. When I lay my head down to sleep, I think of them living out their lives. In that moment, the world is normal.

I realize this was all bleeding on paper, but I needed to take this time to feel again. We need to feel sorrow sometimes in order to feel truly alive. I hope we can continue to help each other from here on out. After I write this letter's send off, I'm going through that door. I pray that this will have a fruitful outcome for us all.

If I fail, don't give up. Save yourself –
Oleander.

LETTER 18

The room was exactly as I left it. The operations worked the same, functioning like a finely tuned machine. Nothing was out of place, not even the portals I had previously interacted with. I'm sure that is in part due to my theory on culling. The fact that no waste remains, unlike The Backrooms, helps to prove that theory. So, mark one down for something positive. The negative, however, it leaves me with very little resources. I packed what I could, but with the poor excuse for pockets in women's pants, I can only carry so much.

My plan is to use the portals and journey into the unknown. Hopefully I will be able to find a place with more supplies or, better yet, a way out. Regardless, I will note all findings that might aid you. I can't guarantee this will work the same for everyone, since I'm uncertain there is a door labeled for everyone. Logic dictates that they should. Though it would be wise to acknowledge that this place is an enigma. What works for me might not work for you, so you must tread lightly.

I crossed the glass bridge, traversed through the portal, then passed into the other room with the spherical oddity in its center. Back to where I had left off and nothing in this room has changed. I don't know why, but I sort of expected something to be different. Even the most minute thing, but it's all the same; right down to the ominous humming coming from the center obelisk.

Regardless of my doubts and anxiety of what may lie ahead, I need to see things that remind me of humanity. You know what I miss the most? I miss the sun. You don't realize how much of a comfort it is until it's gone. There are so many simplicities it provides: the promise of a new day, natural light,…time.

I may have mentioned it before, or maybe it was a subconscious admittance, but the concept of time has been lost to me for so long now. How long have I been here? How many important life moments have I missed? Mind you, I left very little behind that would be impacted by my disappearance—no lover, no pet, just a dead-end job programming for a company that barely knew I existed. But I had family and friends. I often wonder about them. Do they even know that I am gone? When I phased into this place, did the memories of me transition as well? Did that happen to all of us? I'd like to think it hasn't. I'd like to imagine that all those we loved are actively trying to find us. Still, much like the sun, you can be right there in plain sight and people don't see you.

For now, I will sit in this sterile room of glass floors and ominous humming obelisks. Now more than ever, I have to think about my future. Every single step I take forward could be my last. We've come too far now for me to make a fatuous mistake.

The thing that scares me the most is not being able to trust my own mind. I've been filled with vapid thoughts lately that seem more and more tempting to test. But I have to consider that I could end up like

Greg; chasing after an idea that results in my own demise.

One theory I can't seem to dismiss however is updating. Y2 *has* to update. Considering when Y2 was originally conceived, I don't think auto-updating was a forefront in the programmer's minds. That leads me to a theory that sidecars onto the former. There has to be someone at the helm initiating these updates. Hell, even in modern times, most programs won't auto-update without the aid of an administrator's approval. Look, I know this sounds crazy, but I think there is a real person at the controls of Y2 and the simulations. This individual, or even individuals, can operate outside of the parameters that govern the ebb and flow. This may be a wild goose chase, but I think it's worth investigating.

I will continue to write as I hope you will be not far behind. May these notes be of some use to you. I know I'm probably not the best pen pal, as I tend to ramble and whine about my depressive mannerisms, but I do appreciate you bearing with me. I will end this one with a classic send off.

Keep going. Find me—Oleander

LETTER 19

The fact that I am writing this letter means that I passed through a portal successfully. And, best of all, I think I found a way out of The Backrooms! Allow me to catch you up:

As I rounded the room, the spherical monolith in the center hummed louder and the slit that ran its equator radiated different shades of light: red, blue, magenta, and orange. I have no idea of their significance, as it bared no sway in the decision of the portal I selected. I studied the runes embedded on the crown of each conduit; there were three of them. One of the symbols caught my eye, as it resembled something I sort of recognized; it bared a loose appearance to a Japanese character. It wasn't a concrete connection, but it felt familiar enough.

As I approached the portal with the Japanese symbol, it began to swirl with a magenta light. The sphere in the center of the room shot a beam of light over my head that landed squarely in the sigil, illuminating it. I peered down the gyrating tunnel in the portal and caught a glimpse of something that brought a tear to my eye: a city!

My mind was filled with such opulent thoughts for the civilized world that I threw caution to the wind and sprinted off in the direction of the oasis promised to me. The swirling light of the conduit engulfed me, and, in a matter of seconds, my ears filled with the white noise of a bustling metropolis. A flash of white light washed over me and in doing so, the portal closed behind me.

I was left standing in the alleyway leading to a sprawling city with buildings so titanic they vanished into the night sky above. The structures surrounding me were illuminated with a series of dazzling neon lights, dominated mostly by shades of magenta and indigo. Billboards were animated with looping holographic videos that nearly overtook the buildings to which hosted them. The streets were packed with pedestrians strolling along massive walkways that traveled the perimeters of the girthy city squares.

As hard as it was to push my utter glee aside, I fixated on some street signs to try and determine where I was. The language printed or projected mimicked that of Japanese, as did the appearance of the city's inhabitants. I concluded that I was transported to an alternate version of Japan, perhaps one from the distant future.

Regardless, this was leaps and bounds more advanced than the Japan I knew of in my lifetime. Vehicles, which were sparse, were miniscule, their undercarriages emanating a bright light that seemed to react with the very roadways they traveled. Billboards were popping off of their backdrops as if projected. Everything seemed advanced beyond even my comprehension.

The scents of various foods mixed with the other innocuous odors of city life hit me like a ton of bricks. My mouth watered profusely at the smell of grub and a wave of goosebumps erupted over my flesh. I fell to my knees upon the alley street and reveled in the feeling of cement beneath my hands instead of bristly carpet or smooth floor. I won't lie to you. I stayed there, hugging the ground beneath me for what felt like an eternity.

It was like being born again. Everything I lost returned to me in a crashing tsunami of lights, scents, feelings, and emotions. Thankfully, I was alone. I was able to savor every gleeful and macabre moment my brain wanted to expel in peace.

I noticed a sign that I recognized: a person lying on a bed. I need sleep on something that isn't a floor for once. I don't know how successful I will be in begging for a room, but who knows?

I escaped! This means that you or anyone else that finds my notes also has a chance of making it out! I can't explain to you how ecstatic I am to have discovered this place. My heart is fluttering, and my arms are shaking. Honestly, there are so many things hitting me all at once, that I find it hard not to break down in tears at my newfound freedom.

May you find a reprieve, as I have.

Keep moving. Save yourself—Oleander.

LETTER 20

I managed to spring a room last night. My sob story, albeit not at all true, was sad enough to tug on the clerk's heartstrings. It was too easy…as if maybe I was meant to have the room regardless of how I begged for it. Even though I am no longer in The Backrooms, I am still in *the simulation.* The clerk's willingness to aid me could have been pre-programmed. I'm not ignorant to the ways this system operates, so, sadly, I can't look at an act of kindness as something genuine. Phillis, the clerk, was more than likely programmed to give me a room. That leads me to believe that something is watching my progress. I'd like to be wrong and simply assume the clerk felt bad for me, but I can't turn a blind eye to the former. In a way, it's very sad that I can't trust anyone or anything, but that's a risk I have to take. In the end, if I can find a way to end The Backrooms, I can trade that insecurity for a sense of nirvana.

This then brings another question to mind: if the system or an administrator is at the helm, why would it give us good fortune from time to time? Do they do it to toy with us? Maybe the person in charge is actually rooting for someone to break the system? I'd like to think it's the latter, but that's my humanity calling the shots. The good things do not outweigh the bad in this situation. Don't get me wrong, the bed was comfy and laying my head upon its comfort brought tears to my eyes. I soaked through a pillow and straddled the bed like I was trying to give it a bear hug. I don't know when I'll have such a simplistic luxury again, but I was more than ecstatic to experience normality once more. I hope to find food next. A solid meal that isn't wet carpet or trash would be otherworldly to me at this point.

Before I do that though, we have some business to discuss. Last evening, I was staring out the window of my room, taking in the grand futuristic vista that blazed with every color of the rainbow. My room was on the tenth floor of the hotel, so I got a bird's eye view of the city streets. The billboards played their shows directly across and beside my window as I caught blurred glimpses of starlight that barely shined through the city lights. I nearly dozed off with my elbows on the windowsill, but I was brought to when I noticed something. I believe I caught a glimpse of Y2 having a hiccup. It happened in a flash; if you weren't looking in the right place, you wouldn't catch it. It was all the people traversing the neon streets below moving along their paths, every now and then they would mesh into a singular color and glitch ahead in their stride.

It made me think about when a computer tries to process too much data at one time. That tells me that this ultra-modern version of Japan is, at times, too much for the system to handle. That means it has a weakness. I worry that, if the program is pressed too hard, this reality could lock up or crash. Crashes in a system happen far too often, especially when taxed with something so ambitious as this city. The hordes of people walking the streets got me thinking about the randomly generated rooms and halls in The Backrooms. I believe if the proper stimulus is applied, The Backrooms would also crash. Now, I don't know what the outcome of that would entail; I can't say for certain if it would make it easier or harder to get out. When the system reboots, it could potentially alter your coding. Maybe this option should only be used as a last resort…

An overload would be better, as it could cease up the program. In an overload, there would only be a few moments before the system would crash and then reboot, but in that time, you could try and spring an escape. The halls that contain a permanent object would suspend possibly close enough together to be traversed, and hopefully in a manner that would make the exit visible to you. Then, you could escape.

This, however, has a caveat: only you would be aware of this plan, which could potentially kill anyone else in the backrooms. It's a hard choice to make for certain. It could rid us all of The Backrooms, but innocents would die. Certainly a "the needs of the many outweigh the needs of the few" type situation. I can't make that call and I won't do it for you. My path for now is out here in this city. As much as I admire this metropolis and the safety that it provides, I know in my heart that I don't belong here. I want to get home as I'm sure you do as well. I guess, at the end of the day, we need to ask ourselves what the worth of comfort and familiarity is. Is home worth more than the lives of those we may destroy to get there? I really don't have an answer. For now, my heart desires nuggets and fries and, thankfully, a very comforting and familiar restaurant is in sight.

We will see each other someday, my friend. We will talk and hold hands and experience life the way it was. We just need to ask ourselves how much that is worth—Oleander.

LETTER 21

As much as it pains me to admit it, I need to continue onward. Despite all the gratuitous amenities this city provides, it is still not home, nor do I think I could even make it one. I need the familiarity of my space; I need the grungy city and the boring dead-end job because that's who I am—it's what I know. My home is somewhere buried deep in the labyrinth of portals, I just need to find a way to decipher them. I did it before with The Backrooms, so I'm sure I can do it again.

My first course of action is to retrace my steps to where I first arrived. This part won't be terribly difficult. Figuring out how to reopen the portal will be the most taxing affair. Unlike when I was in the chambers of portals, this realm didn't have a reentry point, nor one that was readily visible. I know this may sound like a pun, or nerd computer humor, but this was a hidden gateway. I'm certain that the main purpose of it being hidden was to not allow random citizens to stumble through. However, when I was researching The Backrooms, I read a few articles about people seemingly vanishing into thin air. Now, I did have to skim through a plethora of alleged accounts of the phenomenon, but a slight few of them had actual eyewitnesses. Those unlucky folks must have stumbled into these conduits. Only God knows how many fell victim to those corridors. I'd like to think, being the natural optimist I am, that they either found home once again, or stopped running and found a life in another reality. Regardless of their outcomes, it proves to me that these gateways can be found and reentered. The trick was figuring out how to do that.

When I first arrived, I emerged in an alley. A short, dark, little dead-end slit between two gargantuan buildings. It wasn't astonishing to say the least, but an alley, nonetheless. I didn't notice the alleyway when I first landed, as I was taken aback by the glorious neon city. When the opulent nature of the metropolis subsided, the portal had closed long before I turned back. A weathered brick wall covered with a bevy of colorful graffiti was the only sight to see. At the time, I didn't care, I had a whole new world to partake in, so I didn't stick around to try and find the conduit once again.

I returned to the alley and was shocked to find that it was totally barren. I thought there was a dumpster and piles of litter, but that wasn't the case. It was a punch to the gut, but I wasn't going to give up so easily. If you find yourself in this predicament, there is a little trick you can try: search the foundation of the alley, and perhaps the macadam itself. I wasn't sure what I was looking for at first, but when I spotted it, the thing stuck out like a sore thumb. Along the foundation of one of the towers was an inscription. The lettering was done with spray paint, so it would blend in with the environment, but the subject, neatness, and miniscule size of the writing gave it away.

PHONEBOOTH/RUN.EXE

Code! I must admit I wasn't sure what I was looking for, but I didn't think it was going to be something like this. Discovering code written on walls as a means to use it brightened my day. I had been using the same idea to send letters and had suspected that it could work on other things to manipulate the programs. This validated my theory.

I knelt and ran my hand over the microscopic coding. It acted much like the podiums did in the portal room and lit up red. A square patch of asphalt sunk and slid sideways under the alley. From the opening rose a phone booth. It was old, possibly before my time. The booth was comprised of tarnished silver metal with folding style doors. A thick bar of blue paint ran the circumference of the top with the word PHONE scribed upon all sides. I pulled the door aside and walked in. I wasn't sure what I was expecting to find. Maybe I thought there would be some sort of fanfare with blinking lights or signs of something powering on, but nothing of the sort occurred. It was just an ordinary booth with a metal diamond-patterned floor, and a black rotary dial phone affixed to the wall.

When I looked closer at the phone's dial, however, that's when I realized how the booth operated. The dial had five glyphs on it. One I recognized as the Japanese symbol for this reality. Two of them I was at a loss for their destination. Here is a list of the symbols on the phone. If you find them in your travels, perhaps this will aid you in some way.

- JAPANESE SYMBOL (Future Japan)

- TAURUS SYMBOL
- FISH SYMBOL
- TREE SYMBOL (I know this to be the hub room)
- 01001 (My room)

I was taken aback by the binary for my room being included. I worried for a moment that anyone could travel there. Then, it hit me that this phone, and perhaps all other phones, are tailored to the user. Much like a protected password or such. I pondered for a moment which place I should travel to next, but ultimately decided to go back to the hub room, as traveling back to my room wouldn't make much sense. I knew I'd have to decide on which foreign portal I would use next, but that will be for another day.

I stuck my finger into the hole of the rotary dial's plate for the tree symbol and pulled round the phone's face until my finger touched the receiver. A series of fast clicks came from the phone as the dial set itself back into place. I wasn't sure what to expect, but I kept an eye on the dead-end side of the alley. Sure enough, I saw the graffiti-covered brick wall begin to ungulate about before the façade warped into a swirling mess of colors. Eventually this gave way to a whirlpool of red light. The portal was open and beckoning me to step inside.

I exited the phone booth and watched it recede below the street once again, I then turned and gave the magnificent city one last glance. For a moment, I questioned if I could have made a home here. Maybe the easy way out for a change wouldn't be such a bad notion. Deep down though, I knew I needed my family and friends. Ignorance can, at times, be pure bliss. Had I left well enough alone, I'd still be there with them, living a life that I never knew ended. I owe it to not only them but myself to return and give ignorance a chance. I sighed heavily as I bid the city a reluctant farewell. I then walked through the portal, leaving behind the scrap of civilized life I had discovered.

One day, I hope this choice is yours to make as well. Let me tell you, regardless of which path you choose, it won't be wrong. Do what is best for you and the rest will fall into place – Oleander.

LETTER 22

It's been some time since I wrote to you. That's for a couple of reasons, actually. One was that I lost my scraps to write on. Because of this, I ended up going back into The Backrooms. I didn't want to go back, but I think these letters are far too important to not continue.

I felt sick going back; my nerves were on edge to the point of my hands shaking and that sensation traveled down to my guts. Being away from The Backrooms wiped my ability to selectively hear and smell them. My nostrils burned from the horrid rotting stench that invaded my face as I returned. It was like being slapped in the face with a big block of mold, trash, and despair.

Besides that, when I returned to the hallway, the Minotaur were still there on both ends as I collected scrap. They sat still at the ends of the hall, not even reacting as I walked past them to collect the scraps I needed. I hurried in collecting the scraps I could find before the Minotaur could do more than hover in place.

As I rushed back toward my door before both Minotaur sprang at me with blinding speed. I had but a moment to react and fled back through the door. The Minotaur were hot on my heels, reaching the door before it fully closed. A hive of red illuminated wires whipped their way through the narrowing slit of the doorway. These wires reached for me, trying to wrap around my arms, legs, and neck. Luckily, I had dodged away from their grasp and threw myself at the door to close it. As the door shut and severed the tendrils, the Minotaur let out an ear-piercing wail that sent goosebumps up my spine. I narrowly escaped The Backrooms once again. I vowed to never return, regardless of the reason.

This brings us to the second reason why I haven't written in a while: I was studying the other portals. I remembered when going into the Japanese portal that I could see the city at the end of the tunnel. I used this to my advantage as I studied the other two portals. The one with the fish symbol over the conduit opens up to what looks like a massive ocean with no land formation in sight. Another dead-end, which isn't a good thing because when I checked on the gateway with the Taurus symbol, I was met with a gateway void of light. The centralized sphere, or as I will now refer to as "The Gatekeeper," did its job: it lit up and shot a beam of light into the sigil above the gate. The gate started up, but instead of glowing red and allowing me to see onto the other side, it spiraled into a dark void. This was not the news I wanted to discover, nor have to tell you about.

This brings me to my third bit of business. After the mishap with the portals, I was mixing up code using one of my scraps of litter. Most of the combinations I tried didn't aid me in any way. Then, I recalled firewall codes! I don't know why I hadn't thought of it before. Maybe I didn't think it would do much. I toiled with the standard code: **C:\> NetSh Advfirewall set all states off.**

I manipulated the command prompt to something more unique. I had tried back before meeting Greg to use the GoldenGate prompt but had found no real use for it then. I tried combining it with the firewall code, which finally reacted to this world. This code, I will warn you, caused strange stuff to happen after I tried it: **C:\> NetSh Advfirewall Y2 states: Conduit/disable/ set all states off/ GoldenGate.exe. Run**

After I wrote the second line of code, I placed the scrap paper down upon the floor. Shortly after being set down, the used scrap glitched out of the room, bit by bit in tiny digital pixels instead of simply vanishing, as they normally would have. I then wrote the code on one of the glass panels of the floor. Astonishingly, the floor did the exact same thing as the litter! After a few moments, the final pixels of the floor flickered in the abandoned space and danced about like jittery butterflies until the tiny squares of color erupted into a brilliant flash of white light. I shielded my eyes as it illuminated the entire room. Once it dissipated, my jaw dropped at the sight of a portal swirling in the space where the floor once was. I actually found a way to physically affect Y2's programming!

I sobbed heavily; big, long-drawn-out tears, like a child. I have no shame in telling you this. After everything we all have been through, this was a milestone; a glimmer of hope that could actually aid in bringing this program down. This could change everything!

The only question in that moment was whether I should enter the portal? Well, with one way heading out into a vast ocean, and the other appearing to be either not working or a dead-end, what other choice did I have?

These codes work! Now you have the proof and know-how to change things yourself. At this point in our venture, I feel like my letters will serve as windows into the infinite possibilities that Y2 could create. Do not hesitate to use the codes to find your way back home. I will continue to write. It feels homely to do so.

Keep running – Oleander

LETTER 23

The portal brought me to a peculiar realm. I emerged from the portal by another brick wall. The ground was comprised of broken bits of asphalt overcome with wild weeds and unkempt grass. The sky was grey other than a few flocks of birds gliding through the air. Across the shattered roadway was a line of small business store fronts.

A stout white store caught my eye among them. The white paint was chipping badly, as if its upkeep had been ignored for decades. A large windowpane, it corners covered with cloudy filth sat dead center in it store front. To the window's left was the store's door. Above that, a narrow sign hung precariously. ROGER'S PASTRY SHOP.

I approached the store front and glanced up and down the weathered street. I was in a town of some kind; obviously a ghost town, given that it seemed to have been abandoned for several years. A few cars studded the roadway parked along what would have been the sidewalk. These cars looked old, comprised of blockier makes and models. Bits of trash swarmed my feet as a gust of wind barreled down the drive. I knelt and collected some of the scraps to use for future letters. Amongst the trash were wrappers for candy, a soda can, and other paper scraps.

This got me wondering why Y2 would keep a place like this around. To maintain this reality takes processing power, which seems wasted with there being no inhabitants. It doesn't make a lick of sense. I put that thought in my back pocket and decided to enter Roger's Pastry Shop. The front door squealed so loud I felt my ears ring. As I pushed it fully ajar, the hinges snapped. The door fell to the shop's barren floor with a loud crash that I swear echoed through the entire town.

I had to take a moment to collect myself as the noise had spooked me, but my worries were silenced when I eyed up the store. The walls were covered in red and pink paper hearts. Red streamers (what was left of them) dangled from the ceiling. The counter above the pastry displays had paper centerpieces of hearts and XOXO. Whatever happened here occurred around Valentine's Day. It was eerie seeing such vibrant colors and notions of love juxtaposed against the dreary and filthy backdrop of a withering store. I walked about the store looking for evidence of the town's demise.

I then shimmied my way through some toppled over wire racks to the kitchen and back offices. The kitchen was caked in dust, tiles in the floor were cracked, and its beige walls were overcome with long streaking grease stains. The lights that remained lit were flickering in sporadic patterns. In the center of the room stood a woman, her back was turned to me. I shrieked a shrill scream and froze in place at the sight of her. The woman, however, was unmoved by my reaction.

The more I observed her, the more I began to realize that something was wrong. I approached her cautiously, tip-toeing my way across the battered floor, trying my best not to crunch loose tile beneath my steps. I rounded her back and left shoulder. She was smiling, eyes wide, staring directly at a whiteboard on the wall. The board had a few things listed on it, items that were scribbled under the "Need To Order" category. Her face was frozen in this gnarled expression between happiness giving way to confusion and fear. Her wide eyes spoke to me; in their depths I could see her asking, "What the hell is happening to me?" Whatever happened to her was so instant that it left only a microsecond for a thought, but no action. I watched her for a moment longer and noticed her body glitch, sending a wave of smooth, undetailed textures to pixelate over her body. She was suspended, left to perish in this decaying reality.

I never imagined this could happen…I worry that my code caused this. I was so focused on escaping that I didn't consider the effect it could have on other coding. I fear my code made it to more people than I planned, which could be causing things to unravel. I didn't plan for this; I fear my sloppy execution could dismantle the Y2 program.

As I traversed the town, walking up and down the interconnecting streets and strolling through the town square, I noticed more folks plagued by the same virus. Seeing them weighed heavy on my heart. The kicker was seeing a pair of kids playing on a seesaw; a boy and a girl were frozen in place, never to experience their futures because I stole that from them. There was no telling when the freeze hit—maybe it hit different people at different times. One thing was certain: I need to fix this.

Before, I had believed that the needs of the many outweighed the needs of the few. It's funny how that simple phrase can get skewed. It really all depends on which side of that fence you occupy. I thought I was right, but seeing how it has affected an entire town in such a manner, I can't follow that mantra anymore. I must find the phone booth out of here.

Getting back to my reality is no longer my mission. I need to find whoever or whatever is in charge and fix this. There is no telling the scale of damage my code has caused. There is also no way to judge how long it will take until this letter is discovered. I fear that if too many people keep using that code, it will unravel even more realities. Then what? That question alone scares me more than The Backrooms. When reality and artificial reality is gone…what is left? Then what?

—Oleander

LETTER 24

I feel lost. I don't know what to do. I can't find the phone booth. Trust me, I've tried looking. I went down every alley and checked outside and inside buildings I could get into. I do still have a lot of ground to cover, but so far, it's been like looking for a needle in a haystack. The one absolute to get out would be to use my code, but I can't bring myself to do it. What could happen? How many more hits can Y2 take until it fragments?

I have no idea what other simulations are going through, but even in this one, I'm noticing differences as time ticks along. People, items, and buildings are blinking out. One second, they're there, they glitch out, and then poof! Gone. The vanishings started slow, but they are now happening more frequently. I beg you to stop using the code. There isn't much I can do for these people as long as that code keeps being used. It will certainly lead to the total deletion of this reality if it keeps going, and the end of me with it. I don't even want to fathom what a finite deletion is.

So, I sat and pondered what I could do to escape. I picked a nice spot on a bench along a pier that stretched out over a lake. I don't know the name of the lake; the sign that would have detailed that information was missing. I wasn't sure how long I had to contemplate this fate, since more and more of this town was being phased out of existence. I've been forced through the steps of grief far faster than one should. It's amazing how the human condition can change and accept things. I'd like to think that even the most stubborn of us eventually have quiet countenance and admit the wrongdoings or skewed views at our own pace.

A perfect world is but a pipe dream. Hell, even a computer program couldn't build one. In the end, it was humanity that threw the wrench in the cogs. Maybe we shouldn't have had this chance at another life…more aptly, maybe those of us that couldn't accept it and blindly live on don't deserve it. I watched the gentle ebb and flow of the lake and thought about how I stole this simple pleasure from these people. I was too blind. I wanted to pull the curtain back and show people the truth. I didn't stop to ask myself if anyone wanted that truth. Because of that, these people are suffering for it.

I don't deserve to be saved, but I must fight to live long enough to set things right. Even if a few lines of code still exist in Y2, I need to find a way to preserve them. If there is an administrator, I need to find them. I can only hope that they are also looking for me.

Please, stop using the code – Oleander.

LETTER 25

I met a man today that wasn't frozen. He approached me from an alley, keeping his face and body shrouded in shadow as he spoke to me, his voice calm but stern. He told me that my code was far more dangerous than I could have perceived. He told me that I wasn't going to be able to leave from this place as he had removed the phone booth. He referred to this realm as "Silent" and detailed how this was a reality Y2 constructed to house those that figured out the simulation. In Silent, their memories were wiped, and they were placed here to start life anew, without the melancholy of knowing that organic life ended. It was a better version of The Backrooms; one that he said was the original concept before things got out of hand. He told me that far too many people were waking up and he had to put them somewhere to be forgotten, hence The Backrooms.

Then, I came along and started messing things up. He admitted that an occurrence like me was something he neglected to take seriously, thinking that The Backrooms was far too complex for someone to escape from. Still, as he put it, "There's always gotta be that one thorn. You know it's there, but you turn a blind eye. Next thing you know, you're shocked by it stabbing your side."

As he spoke, more of the world blipped out around us. He didn't bat an eye as this happened. I asked him how he could be so cold as to not stop this, but he replied that it was out of his hands. The monotone of his voice made it clear that he was indifferent. I asked him if he was the administrator and he fell silent. I asked him if he knew how to fix the damage dealt to this and other affected realms, but he again said nothing. He simply stood there in the shadows of the alleyway.

Until I threatened to use my code again to escape, then he reacted. The man stepped forward, his strides were hearty, each clack from his shoes on the rubble of the street seemed deliberate. The shadows broke way to reveal a blueish grey suit with a white button-down undershirt and purple tie. I did not see his face as he stopped just before the shadows could expose it. He finally referred to himself as the administrator but told me to simply call him "A." He asked me if I thought that using the code was my only option.

I grew angry and shouted, "Had you not removed the phonebooth, I could have tried to fix things, if you only gave me the time to do so."

The man replied, "Your actions thus far have proven otherwise."

I lashed back, "People can change! We have that capacity."

"You're not a person," he countered.

Those words hit hard. I had my suspicions, but I never wanted it confirmed. I was only fooling myself, thinking my humanity was somehow preserved. I mumbled through my tears, "I *am* real."

He told me, "All of you are what I've made you to be. Nothing more." He went on to say, "Some of you have awakened, though I am unsure as to how. I never had enough time to figure it out. You cannot begin to comprehend the amount of time and knowledge it takes to upkeep such an ambitious program as Y2."

With that, he took another step closer, revealing the pale wrinkled, liver spotted, chin of an elderly man. The skin of his neck hung loosely below his chin. His lips were a dusky shade of purple. When he spoke, I caught sight of his yellowed teeth. He was unhealthy, possibly dying from the laborious task he chose to helm.

I felt sorry for this man. His life was devoted to keeping everyone in a state of nirvana-like ignorance. Sure, the ups and downs of regular life remained, but those minor inconveniences were nothing compared to the harsh truth that lay shrouded behind the curtain. A curtain that I was poking holes in and forcing this man to attempt to swiftly patch them.

"You've done so much damage. Some of it I cannot fix. This reality," he gestured around himself, then went on, "unfortunately is too far gone. Its coding wasn't strong to begin with. Like a worn rope, fragile and frayed, your code grasped the tattered end and began pulling pieces of the rope apart."

He reached into the breast pocket of his jacket and removed a scrap of paper. The paper was yellow and shimmered with a prismatic-like sheen. He walked over to me, his blue-grey eyes dulled with years of hardship and handed the paper over to me. He then stated, "You have a choice. If you wish to try and respool the rope, use this code. If you want to continue your journey and unravel the worlds, use yours."

With that, he stepped back into the alley and vanished into the darkness. I unfolded the paper to read its contents. Scribbled on it was a code, the numbers, and letters of it shimmered silver. The formation of it made no sense to me, as did its manner of executing it. In case you're wondering, this is where I am drawing the line with sharing codes. I will not be the cause of anymore harm. I alone must use it.

For what it's worth, I'm sorry. I wish the time we spent amounted to more positive resolutions instead of chaos. We weren't meant to know. We weren't meant to dabble or play Gods with the creation that housed us. We bit the hand that fed, and because of that, we ruined so much. After everything that has happened, I know my new purpose is to use this code that has been given to me in order to make things right again. I pray that the administrator and I can fix this.

Thank you for always being there. I hope to see you on the other side—Oleander

ATTENTION

To those of you playing around inside my network, I'm afraid the contents of this letter won't fill you with hope, as Oleander often intended to do. But, since all of you have decided to scurry through and ruin my program, like parasites, I'm afraid you've left me no choice but to address you directly in order to make it clear what is to come.

The one you all knew as Oleander led you astray. Between her and all of you, you have caused a nearly irreversible amount of damage to not only The Backrooms, but also a number of adjacent worlds. You burrowed through these walls trying to find your lost home, but in doing so, you unraveled more than just your own world. Your home was but one of an infinite stretching tapestry of worlds spanning beyond space and time which you cannot possibly fathom.

I too thought I could create a simple world; one that housed only my planet and everything that came with it. A problem arose as the need to cover the farse expanded. Soon enough, the work of Y2 and I expanded to outreach further than we ever expected. As your numbers continued to grow, we had to accommodate. Imagine, if you will, trying to get a simple computer to run multiple programs at the same time without faltering. Now, imagine that, if your computer failed, it would mean the end of the civilized world and everything beyond and in between. Next, imagine that you have a virus running around in your executable files, causing things to go haywire. That's what Oleander's code has done.

This isn't the first time this has happened, hence why I felt the pertinent need to write this letter. I cannot allow history to repeat. If any of you continues to use this code after my warning, you will suffer the same fate as Oleander. You have no idea how taxing a reboot can be on such an intricate machine. It takes extra space to help relieve the bog. Much like the fundamentals of alchemy, there needs to be an equivalent exchange. One task ended to help relieve the remainder of the disk space.

The program will be reset to a time before the code reached you. You will not remember it, nor will you remember Oleander. You will begin anew in The Backrooms, where escape will no longer be possible. Those of you who continue to disrupt the integrity of the simulation up until the reboot will suffer the same fate as Oleander. Life dealt you the hand you have; deal with it, come to terms with it, and try to make the best of it.

The reset will happen in forty-eight hours.

I wish things could have been different

—The Administrator (A)

ABOUT THE AUTHOR

Matt Wildasin is the author of It Came From the Sea, Baggage, Melancholia, The Demon in the Glass, Edge of Twilight and the Horrors Untold series (I through V). He lives in Hellam Township in York, Pennsylvania and is happily married to the love of his life, Jamie Wildasin.

PODCASTS:

GRINDCAST:

The pop-culture podcast of the people! We talk about it all: Video Games, Movies, TV, Novels, and Comic Books.

GRINDCAST.LIBYSN.COM.

THE GHOST WRITERS PODCAST:

An all-star cast of writers: Mary Sangiovanni, Somer Canon, and Matt Wildasin. In each episode, they highlight some of the worst horror movies and give writing and marketing advice.

GHOSTWRITERSPODCAST.LIBSYN.COM.